I Am ...

A Children's Mantra Book

Written By: Cassandra Mary Bauer

Magical Illustration By: Melissa Van Der Veen

WELCOME TO THE
WORLD OF

NOWLEVELUP

WHERE **WE** ARE THE **HEROES**
OF
OUR **OWN** STORIES
NOW.

Written/Art Direction By:
Cassandra Mary Bauer
Founder of NOWLEVELUP
www.NOWLEVELUP.com

Magical Illustration By:
Melissa Van Der Veen
www.mayhem.studio

I Am Magic

a Children's Mantra Book

i remember...

I was seven years old when we got our first family dog. His name was Doc. Throughout the years we developed a very special relationship, one where we would wander into other worlds for hours and get lost in play and imagination.

As I got older I realized the blessing that he had given me. He empowered me to always believe in something more than meets the eye and to know I was never alone.

When I was old enough to get a dog of my own, I found Magic. Magic brought the play and wonder back into my life and reminded me of my deepest purpose in this world—to spread Love, to empower others to believe in magic, and to help them know they are not alone on their journey.

My intention behind creating this book is to help adults and their little ones connect deeply as they play in the magic together.

remember to remember...

this book is dedicated to all magicians,

Big -n- Little.

this is a reminder that we are never too old or too young to remember the magic that lives inside of us.

We deserve to always play in the sandbox.

We deserve to be the perfect mirrors for one another.

We all deserve to own our magic NOW.

How to use this book:

show up as the perfect mirrors for one another.

"It's just that simple."

Once Upon

Cass

A Time ...

Magic

Until one day she opened...

Little Magician Mantra:

I AM FULL OF MAGIC!

the door to magic!

Big Magician Mantra:

YOU ARE FULL OF MAGIC!

So their imagination was where they began to stay!

Big Magician:

YOU ARE THE KEY!

YOU DESERVE TO PLAY!

They began to paint the world

with color...

Little Magician:

I AM FULL OF COLOR!

And created a universe of wonder!

Big Magician:

YOU ARE ART!

When it was too cold to go outside...

When it was

too hot

to bear...

They hopped on a vine and flew through the air!

Even when Cass had to go to school...

Little Magician:

I AM CAPABLE!

She would always bring Magic
as a secret tool!

Big Magician:

YOU ARE CAPABLE!

Magic never let her fall apart!

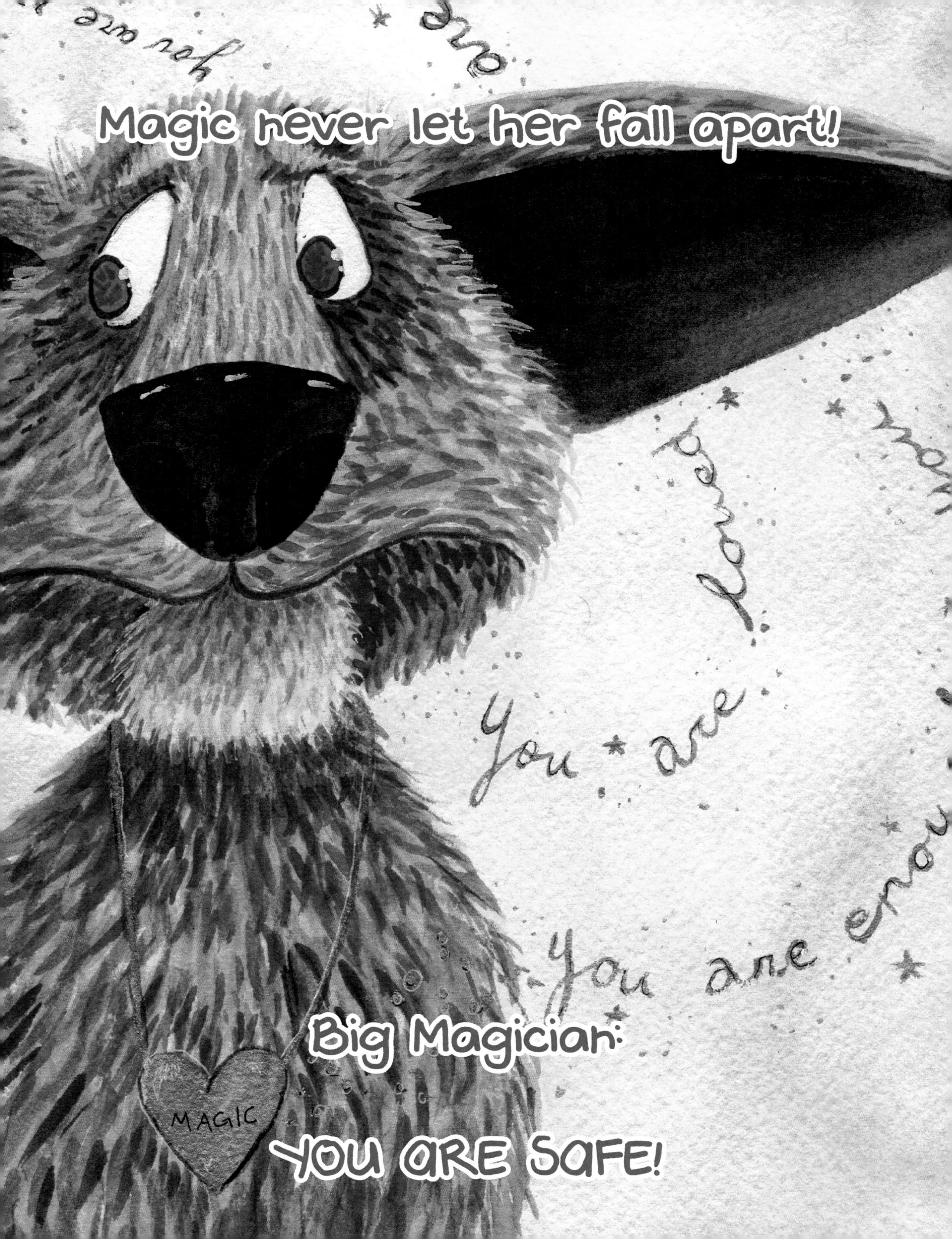

Big Magician:

YOU ARE SAFE!

One day magic woke up to realize...

He wouldn't always be around to be her guide...

So he made sure to give her his heart of gold...

NOW...

when magic had to depart, this was the fairytale start...

WHERE...

Cass never felt like she was wandering ALONE...

She had finally found HOME.

"I am not alone"

"I am HOME!"

together:

I
Am
Magic

THE END

this is just the
BEGINNING
of your magical journey

MEET the wanderers

Cass & Magic

"We choose to get lost in the magic of this LIFE over and over again to find more COLOR -n- LOVE to bring to you.

stay in your heart and you will never go wrong."

Sat Nam,

Cass and Mag

GRATITUDE

thank you for waking up every morning
and
saying 'yes' to this experience.

i see you,
i acknowledge you
-n-
i love you.

A very special thank you to my family

Abbe Bauer
Blakie Bauer
Dude Bauer
Magic Bauer
Marshall Bauer
Jason Levinson
Sophie Lauter

And, all my angels for reminding me of my
souls purpose every day.

I love you forever and always,

iUniverse
1663 Liberty Drive
Bloomington, IN 47403
www.iuniverse.com
844-349-9409

ISBN: 978-1-6632-0909-2 (sc)
ISBN: 978-1-6632-0910-8 (e)
ISBN: 978-1-6632-0908-5 (hc)

Library of Congress Control Number: 2020917500

iUniverse rev. date: 07/27/2021

Made in United States
North Haven, CT
05 December 2022

27948260R00024